CORDUROY

Also by Don Freeman

BEADY BEAR   COME AGAIN, PELICAN

MOP TOP   SKI PUP

FLY HIGH, FLY LOW   THE TURTLE AND THE DOVE

THE NIGHT THE LIGHTS WENT OUT   DANDELION

NORMAN THE DOORMAN   A RAINBOW OF MY OWN

SPACE WITCH   THE GUARD MOUSE

CYRANO THE CROW

By Lydia and Don Freeman

PET OF THE MET

CORDUROY

Story and Pictures by Don Freeman

THE VIKING PRESS / NEW YORK

To Sally Elizabeth Kildow
and Patrick Steven Duff Kildow,
who know how a bear feels about buttons

Pic Bk
Trade 670–24133–4   VLB 670–24134–2
4 5 6 7 8   74 73 72 71 70

Corduroy is a bear who once lived in the toy department of a big store. Day after day he waited with all the other animals and dolls for somebody to come along and take him home.

The store was always filled with shoppers buying all sorts of things, but no one ever seemed to want a small bear in green overalls.

Then one morning a little girl stopped and looked straight into
Corduroy's bright eyes.

"Oh, Mommy!" she said. "Look! There's the very bear I've always
wanted."

"Not today, dear." Her mother sighed. "I've spent too much already.
Besides, he doesn't look new. He's lost the button to one of his
shoulder straps."

Corduroy watched them sadly as they walked away.

"I didn't know I'd lost a button," he said to himself. "Tonight I'll go and see if I can find it."

Late that evening, when all the shoppers had gone and the doors were shut and locked, Corduroy climbed carefully down from his

shelf and began searching everywhere on the floor for his lost
button.

Suddenly he felt the floor moving under him! Quite by accident he
had stepped onto an escalator—and up he went!

"Could this be a mountain?" he wondered. "I think I've always wanted to climb a mountain."

He stepped off the escalator as it reached the next floor, and there,
before his eyes, was a most amazing sight—

tables and chairs and lamps and sofas, and rows and rows of beds.
"This must be a palace!" Corduroy gasped. "I guess I've always
wanted to live in a palace."

He wandered around admiring the furniture.
"This must be a bed," he said. "I've always wanted to sleep in a bed." And up he crawled onto a large, thick mattress.

All at once he saw something small and round.
"Why, here's my button!" he cried. And he tried to pick it up. But, like all the other buttons on the mattress, it was tied down tight.

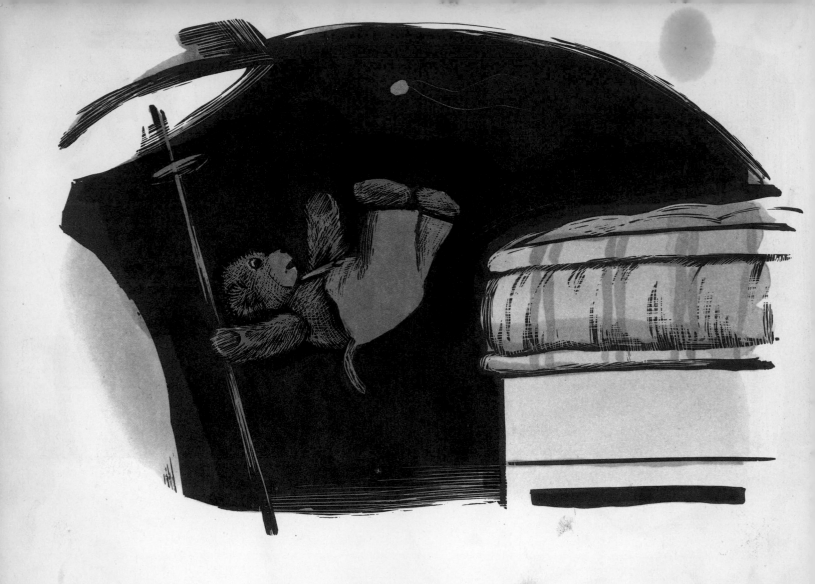

He yanked and pulled with both paws until POP! Off came the
button—and off the mattress Corduroy toppled,

bang into a tall floor lamp. Over it fell with a crash!

19

Corduroy didn't know it, but there was someone else awake in the store. The night watchman was going his rounds on the floor above. When he heard the crash he came dashing down the escalator.

"Now who in the world did that!" he exclaimed. "Somebody must be hiding around here!"

He flashed his light under and over sofas and beds until he came to
the biggest bed of all. And there he saw two fuzzy brown ears
sticking up from under the cover.

"Hello!" he said. "How did *you* get upstairs?"

The watchman tucked Corduroy under his arm and carried him
down the escalator

and set him on the shelf in the toy department with the other
animals and dolls.

Corduroy was just waking up when the first customers came into
the store in the morning. And there, looking at him with a wide,
warm smile, was the same little girl he'd seen only the day before.

26

"I'm Lisa," she said, "and you're going to be my very own bear. Last night I counted what I've saved in my piggy bank and my mother said I could bring you home."

"Shall I put him in a box for you?" the saleslady asked.

"Oh, no thank you," Lisa answered. And she carried Corduroy home in her arms.

She ran all the way up four flights of stairs, into her family's apartment, and straight to her own room.

Corduroy blinked. There was a chair and a chest of drawers, and alongside a girl-size bed stood a little bed just the right size for him. The room was small, nothing like that enormous palace in the department store.

"This must be home," he said. "I *know* I've always wanted a home!"

Lisa sat down with Corduroy on her lap and began to sew a button
on his overalls.

"I like you the way you are," she said, "but you'll be more
comfortable with your shoulder strap fastened."

"You must be a friend," said Corduroy. "I've always wanted a friend."

"Me too!" said Lisa, and gave him a big hug.